MONSTAR
Finds A Home

STEVE COLE
Illustrated by PETE WILLIAMSON

First published in Great Britain in 2014
by Orion Children's Books
a division of the Orion Publishing Group Ltd
Orion House
5 Upper Saint Martin's Lane
London WC2H 9EA
An Hachette UK Company

1 3 5 7 9 10 8 6 4 2

Text © Steve Cole 2014
Illustrations © Pete Williamson 2014
Inside design: www.hereandnowdesign.com

ISBN 978 1 4440 0971 2

A catalogue record for this book is available from the British Library.

Printed and bound in China

www.orionbooks.co.uk

For my Amy

Contents

Chapter One   11

Chapter Two   21

Chapter Three   29

Chapter Four   39

Chapter Five   45

Chapter Six   55

Chapter Seven   65

Chapter One

Jon and Jen wanted a pet. Their parents had promised them one **ages** ago.

The trouble was, Jen and Jon's
mum and dad were mad scientists.

They were busy doing crazy experiments the whole time, so nothing normal ever happened.

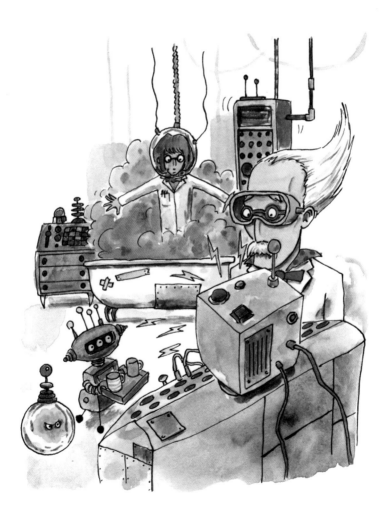

"Can we have cornflakes for breakfast, Dad?" asked Jon.

"No. Mum set fire to the cornflakes," said Dad. "But I just invented green porridge. I bet it's really nice!"

It wasn't.

"Can you drive
us to school,
Mum?"
asked Jen.

"No. Dad blew up
the car," said Mum.
"But I just invented
flying rocket-pants
that will whizz you
to school in half
the time!"

They didn't.

"Can we have a pet?" asked Jon and Jen. "You promised you'd get us one. You promised!"

"Oh, all right," said Dad. "Tell you what – Mum and I will **invent** you a pet!"

Jen and Jon looked at each other…
and gulped!

Chapter Two

Strange noises could be heard
from Mum and Dad's secret lab.

Clang! Oof! Blupp!!!
Gub-a-lub-a-lub-a-lub.
"Whatever are they doing?"
Jen wondered.

Then Mum and Dad came in
holding a big bundle in a blanket.
"There," said Mum. "Your very
own pet!"

Jen gasped. "Is it a dog?"
"No."

"A cat?" asked Jon.
"No."

"A rabbit?"

The bundle growled.
"Definitely not," said Dad.

Suddenly, a fluffy thing the size of a puppy wriggled out from under the blanket! She had pale green fur, with a brown patch in the shape of a star over one eye.

Waving her arms, waggling
her tail, she jumped up, did a
somersault in mid air…

…and landed head-first on the
carpet.

"Uff!" said the fluffy thing. "Eeek!" cried Jen and Jon. Mum beamed. "You now have your own pet Monstar!"

Chapter Three

Jen and Jon soon learned lots about their new pet.

They learned that…

1. Monstar liked licking people. Very much.

2. Monstar's favourite thing was dressing up.

3. Monstar actually *liked* green porridge. She could eat buckets and buckets.

4. Monstar grew bigger very, very quickly.

5. Monstar did not like bath time.

Jen and Jon loved Monstar very much. She was snuggly. She gave the best rides. She was fun.

But Mum and Dad were not so happy.
"She's grown so big," Dad said.
"She's broken five beds already."

"She keeps digging holes in the garden," Mum moaned.
"I have to mix fifty buckets of green porridge for her each day," Dad grumbled.

"She's going to have to stay outside
from now on. We've just about
had enough!"

Chapter Four

Before bedtime, Jen and Jon went out into the garden to see Monstar.

She was covered in mud and busy digging another hole in the lawn.

"You'd better stop that, Monstar," said Jen. "You've made Mum and Dad mad."

"This is serious," John said.
"Ear-ious?" Monstar licked Jon's ear.
"Serious, not ear-ious." Jen hugged
her pet and sighed.

Monstar kicked some mud into
the hole she'd dug, brushed down
her tutu and lay on the grass.
"Me try and be good."

"Thank you, Monstar." Jen felt
sad as she and Jon waved bye-bye.
"See you tomorrow."

Chapter Five

That night, Jen and Jon were woken by Mum and Dad shouting…

"I can't stop it!"
"It's pouring out of the window!"

"What's going on?" said Jon
sleepily.
"It's going to flood the whole
town!" Dad cried.
Jen got up and went to the
window…

She gasped. A stream of green
porridge was spreading across the
garden!

Jen and Jon ran downstairs. They found Mum and Dad in a flap.

"I was inventing a green-porridge maker," cried Dad. "I tested it, and it works – but now I can't turn it off!"

"The town will be struck by a tidal wave of porridge," Mum sobbed.

Jen and Jon ran outside in their pyjamas to see. The porridge pond was glowing sickly green in the moonlight – and growing larger.

"If it reaches the end of the garden and spills down the hill," said Jon, "the town will drown in porridge!"

Jen gasped. "It isn't reaching the end of the garden. It's pouring into the holes that Monstar made!"

"Hooray!" Jon cheered. "But those holes will soon fill up..."
Jen smiled. "I have an idea."

She ran to where Monstar lay
curled up on the ground, snoring.
"Wake up, Monstar. We need you!"

Chapter Six

The furry monster opened one eye.

"Jen! Jon!" She jumped up and did a twirl. "Licks! Licks!"

"No time for that," said Jen.
"There's a porridge emergency!
Are you hungry?"
"Hungry?" said Monstar. Then she
noticed the porridge, and smiled.

"Mmmm! Early breakfast!"
She dived in with a splash
and got guzzling. "Yum, yum,
Yummmm!"

Jon stared. "She can't eat it all…
can she?"
"I bet she can!" Jen crossed her
fingers, as Monstar gulped down
and gobbled up the porridge.

More and more came pouring out from the crazy machine in the lab…

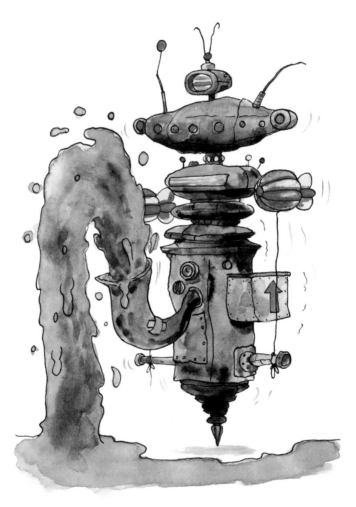

But thanks to Monstar's amazing appetite, the porridge level kept going down!

Finally – "I've done it!" yelled Dad. "I've stopped the porridge maker."

"Good!" Jon shouted. "Because the porridge **eater** has stopped too!"

"Full up!" Monstar flopped on her back with a happy burp.

The children gave her the biggest hug.

Chapter Seven

"You clever girl, Monstar!" Mum cheered. "You saved us all from a porridge disaster!"

"Thank you, Monstar," said Dad. "I'm sorry I was cross about you digging holes. They came in very handy."

"They're not holes now," said Jon.
"They are porridge wells!"

Dad laughed. "I'll fill them up every day. Monstar can eat all she likes!"

"Really?" said Monstar.

"Yes," Mum said. "And since you're so good at digging, you can make a lovely big burrow for yourself too – underground!"

Monstar did a little dance of joy.
"It'll be a proper home for you,
Monstar!" said Jon. "It will be
warm and cosy."

"And we will come and play with you there," said Jen, hugging Monstar tight. "Every single day!"

And do you know what?
That's exactly what they did.

What are you going to read next?

Have more adventures with Horrid Henry,

and travel
the world
with
Miranda the Explorer.

Play clever tricks with Twit,

spend
Mondays at Monster School,

and even
brave
The Dragon's Dentist . . .

Learn how love is just like a Woolly Hat,

dance under The Little Nut Tree,

take home Monstar, the best pet ever,

and have an extra-special Mr Monkey birthday party!

Enjoy all the Early Readers.

Look out for more Early Readers
by Steve Cole and Pete Williamson

Monstar the Superhero

Monstar Makes A Wish

And don't miss

TWIT

by Steve Cole and Jane Porter

There was once a little owl who wasn't very wise at all. This owl was called Twit and his brothers played all sorts of tricks on him.

Sign up for **the orion star** newsletter
for all the latest children's book news,
plus activity sheets, exclusive competitions,
author interviews, pre-publication extracts
and more.

www.orionbooks.co.uk/newsletters

Follow  @the_orionstar on 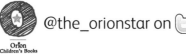.